MOUSE MATH

# IF THE SHOE FITS

by **Jennifer Dussling** • Illustrated by **Deborah Melmon**

THE KANE PRESS / NEW YORK

*For Judy Donnelly, my mentor and friend—J.D.*

Acknowledgments: We wish to thank the following people for their helpful advice and review of the material contained in this book: Susan Longo, Early Childhood and Elementary School Teacher, Mamaroneck, NY; and Rebeka Eston Salemi, Kindergarten Teacher, Lincoln School, Lincoln, MA.

Special thanks to Susan Longo for providing the Fun Activities in the back of this book.

Library of Congress Cataloging-in-Publication Data

Dussling, Jennifer.
If the shoe fits / by Jennifer Dussling ; illustrated by Deborah Melmon.
pages cm. — (Mouse math)
Summary: Albert the mouse finds the perfect clubhouse for his playroom—a human shoe—
but first he must measure it and avoid Groucho the cat.
ISBN 978-1-57565-800-1 (library reinforced binding : alk. paper) —
ISBN 978-1-57565-801-8 (pbk. : alk. paper)
[1. Mice—Fiction. 2. Measurement—Fiction.] I. Melmon, Deborah, illustrator. II. Title.
PZ7.D943If 2015
[E]—dc23
2015012883
eISBN: 978-1-57565-802-5

1 3 5 7 9 10 8 6 4 2

First published in the United States of America in 2015 by Kane Press, Inc.
Printed in the United States of America

Book Design: Edward Miller

Mouse Math is a registered trademark of Kane Press, Inc.

Visit us online at **www.kanepress.com**

Like us on Facebook
facebook.com/kanepress

Follow us on Twitter
@KanePress

Dear Parent/Educator,

"I can't do math." Every child (or grownup!) who says these words has at some point along the way felt intimidated by math. For young children who are just being introduced to the subject, we wanted to create a world in which math was not simply numbers on a page, but a part of life—an adventure!

Enter Albert and Wanda, two little mice who live in the walls of a People House. Children will be swept along with this irrepressible duo and their merry band of friends as they tackle mouse-sized problems and dilemmas (and sometimes *cat-sized* problems and dilemmas!).

Each book in the **MOUSE MATH**® series provides a fresh take on a basic math concept. The mice discover solutions as they, for instance, use position words while teaching a pet snail to do tricks or count the alarmingly large number of friends they've invited over on a rainy day—and, lo and behold, they are doing math!

Math educators who specialize in early childhood learning have applied their expertise to make sure each title is as helpful as possible to young children—and to their parents and teachers. Fun activities at the ends of the books and on our website encourage kids to think and talk about math in ways that will make each concept clear and memorable.

As with our award-winning Math Matters® series, our aim is to captivate children's imaginations by drawing them into the story, and so into the math at the heart of each adventure. It is our hope that kids will want to hear and read the **MOUSE MATH** stories again and again and that, as they grow up, they will approach math with enthusiasm and see it as an invaluable tool for navigating the world they live in.

Sincerely,

*Joanne Kane*

Joanne E. Kane
Publisher

Albert grabbed his sister's arm. "Wanda, what's that?"

Albert and Wanda were coming back from picking berries in the People yard. Something strange was in the grass ahead of them.

They crept closer.

It was big. It was red. It was . . .

It was a People shoe!

Albert jumped up and down. This shoe was the best thing EVER! What was it doing outside? It was right where Groucho the cat could find it!

Groucho had beat Albert to some great stuff before.
A huge striped feather. A pink rubber ball. A dropped
hotdog bun. But not this time!

"Wanda, we have to take that shoe home!" Albert said.
"We can put it in the playroom. It'll be our clubhouse!"

Wanda looked at the shoe. "It *would* be a perfect clubhouse," she said. "But it's big and heavy, and the playroom is far away. I don't want to get there and find out it doesn't fit!"

"So?" Albert said. "We can measure it first."

"We don't have a ruler," Wanda pointed out.

"I have an idea!" Albert said. "I'll use my feet to measure it."

Albert walked next to the shoe. He put one foot in front of the other. He counted "One, two, three . . ." until he reached the end. "It's twelve mouse feet long," he said.

**12 Albert feet**

Wanda nodded. "I'll double-check." She measured with *her* feet. "It's ten mouse feet long."

Albert looked at his mouse foot. He looked at Wanda's mouse foot. "Hey! Your feet are bigger than mine. That's why we got different numbers."

**10 Wanda feet**

"Let's measure it with something else," Wanda said.

"I know," Albert said. He reached into his backpack. "CHEESE!" He held up a cheese stick.

Albert measured the shoe. It was exactly eight cheese sticks long.

**8 cheese sticks**

Albert and Wanda crossed the yard. They scurried along next to the fence, around the flowerpots, and over the log pile. Finally they reached home.

13

"Now we need to measure the playroom," Wanda said.

Albert took the cheese stick from his bag.

Wanda looked at it. It seemed shorter. "Albert," she asked, "did you *eat* part of the cheese stick?"

"I got hungry," he said.

"What else can we measure with?" Wanda asked. "It has to be one size. Not like mouse feet! And it has to stay the same size. Not like a cheese stick!"

Albert thought for a moment. "Paper clips!" he said.

Albert had a paper clip collection. The purple ones were his favorites. They were all the exact same size. He ran and got them.

Albert measured. The playroom was seven paper clips long.

Albert and Wanda peeked outside. No Groucho.

They hurried over the log pile, around the flowerpots, and along the fence. The shoe was right where they had left it.

"Whew! I was afraid Groucho would find it," Albert said.

Wanda measured the shoe. It was five paper clips long.
It would fit in the playroom . . . with two paper clips to
spare!

Albert picked up the heel. Wanda picked up the toe. They carried the shoe along the fence. They carried it around the flowerpots. They carried it to the log pile.

Albert and Wanda stopped to catch their breath.
That shoe was heavy! Then they climbed to the
top of the log pile.

Albert looked down and saw—

GROUCHO!

Groucho looked up and saw—
Albert and Wanda!

Albert shrieked! Wanda shrieked!

They dropped the shoe.

The shoe tumbled off the log pile . . .

. . . and hit Groucho on the nose!

Groucho yowled! He ran away as fast as his cat feet could run.

Albert shook his paw at Groucho. "Take that, cat!"
he cried.

Albert and Wanda raced down the side of the woodpile
and grabbed the shoe. They ran as fast as their mouse
feet could run.

They crammed the shoe through the back door.
They crammed it through the playroom door.

They put it between the bookshelf and the ball hoop.

It fit perfectly!

Wanda and Albert's mouse clubhouse was *mousetastic*!
Albert popped his head out of the toe hole. Wanda
climbed the shoelace. Albert crawled through the middle.
Wanda sat on the tongue and read a book.

"It just needs one more thing," Wanda said.

On the side of the shoe, she painted,
"NO CATS ALLOWED!"

# FUN ACTIVITIES

*If the Shoe Fits* supports children's understanding of **nonstandard units of measurement**, an important topic in early math learning. Use the activities below to extend the math topic and to support children's early reading skills.

## ENGAGE

▶ Remind the children that the cover of a book can often tell them a lot about the story inside. Ask the children: *What do you think this story is about?* Record their predictions and refer back to them at the end of the reading.

▶ Ask the children: *Who knows what a clubhouse is? Who can describe what one looks like? Are all clubhouses the same?*

▶ Now it's time to read the story out loud and find out what happens to Albert and Wanda and their new, special clubhouse.

## LOOK BACK

▶ After reading the story to the children, ask: *Who remembers some of the problems that Albert and Wanda ran into in this story?* Make a list of all the problems the children can recall. Problems may include: 1) Albert and Wanda didn't know if the shoe would fit in their playroom. 2) They didn't know what to use to measure the shoe. 3) Albert ate part of the cheese stick. 4) Groucho, the cat, spotted them on the log pile!

▶ Now discuss how each of these problems was resolved in the story. Record children's responses next to each problem listed.

▶ Ask the children to help make a list of all the items in the story that were used to measure the shoe. Ask: *Which of these items worked the best? Why?* Ask: *Do you think Albert and Wanda could have used their feet to measure the playroom? How might they have done this?*

## TRY THIS!

**Let's Go Tightrope Measuring!**

▶ Place a long strip of wide masking tape or duct tape on the floor in an open area. Next, have the children remove their shoes and ask them to become *TIGHTROPE WALKERS*, as one would see in the circus.

▶ Each child is to take turns counting how many "feet" long the strip of tape is as he or she places one foot in front of the other (and tries NOT to fall!). For an even greater comparison of measurements, the adults in the room may also try this! Record everyone's results on a large sheet of paper. Review the findings.

▶ Ask the children what they notice from the results. *Were all the numbers the same? Who had the highest number of feet recorded? Who had the lowest number? Ask: Why were the measurements different for different people?*

**Let's Measure Some More!**

▶ Trace each child's right foot onto a sheet of cardboard. Cut it out and label it with the child's name. Demonstrate how to measure using a cardboard foot. Encourage the children to measure different items around the room using their "feet." Items may include tables, bookcases, rugs, etc.

▶ Have children record their results on a sheet of paper. Encourage them to draw what they have measured, with the measurement written alongside. Have them share their results with a partner when they are done. Happy measuring!

## THINK!

**Design Your Own "Dream" Clubhouse!**

▶ Begin by reminding the children that all clubhouses look different. Ask the children to think about these questions: *What do you want your clubhouse to look like? How big or small do you want it to be? Where would you build it? In a tree? In your house? What would you include in your clubhouse?*

▶ Provide children with construction paper, crayons, markers, and rulers (to help form straight lines). Encourage them to use their imaginations. As the children complete their designs, have them write about the clubhouses on large index cards. Remind them to include as many details about their designs as possible.

▶ When all the Dream Clubhouse designs and their descriptions are completed, display them somewhere for others to appreciate and enjoy!

◆ **FOR MORE ACTIVITIES** ◆

visit www.kanepress.com/mouse-math-activities